The River and the Rain

The Lord's Prayer

Bijou Le Tord

*A Doubleday Book
for Young Readers*

A Doubleday Book for Young Readers
Published by
Delacorte Press
Bantam Doubleday Dell Publishing Group, Inc.
1540 Broadway
New York, New York 10036

Library of Congress Cataloging in Publication Data
Le Tord, Bijou.
The river and the rain : the Lord's prayer / Bijou Le Tord.
p.   cm.
"A Doubleday Book for Young Readers."
ISBN 0-385-32034-5
1. Lord's prayer—Paraphrases, English.   2. Lord's prayer—Juvenile
literature.   [1. Lord's prayer.]   I. Title.   BV232.L47   1994
226.9'605209—dc20   93-20730   CIP   AC

Typography by Lynn Braswell
Manufactured in Italy
September 1994
10   9   8   7   6   5   4   3   2   1

The following animals of the rain forest appear in *The River and the Rain:*

Front jacket: scarlet macaw, *page 5:* toucan, *page 6:* catfish, *page 7:* dragonfly,
page 9: green and red parrots, *page 10:* beetles, *page 11:* leaf-cutting ants, *pages 14
and 15:* pacu fish, *page 21:* tamandua anteater, *page 28:* giant otters, *page 29:* herons,
page 30: jaguar, *page 31:* tapir, *back jacket:* Franquet's fruit bats and tambaqui fish.

For Kenna with love

Our
Father
in
Heaven,

Be

praised!

for

your

loving

ways.

Your

Kingdom

come.

Your will be done

on

earth,

as it is

in

Heaven.

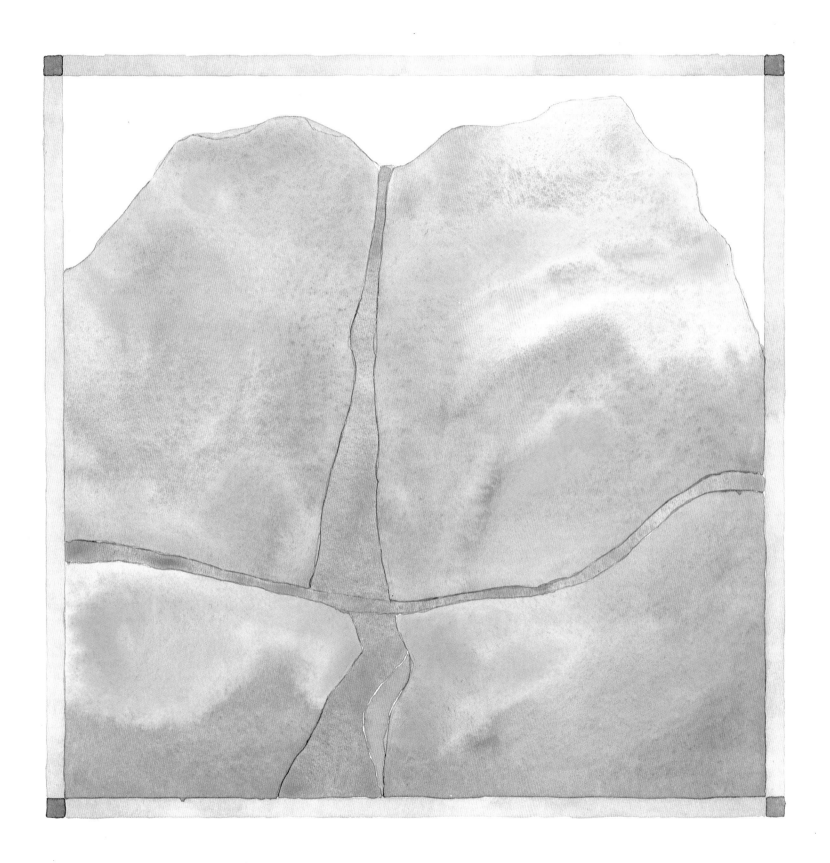

Give
us
food

for

each

day.

And
forgive
us
our
wicked
ways,

as

we

forgive

the

wicked

ways

of

others.

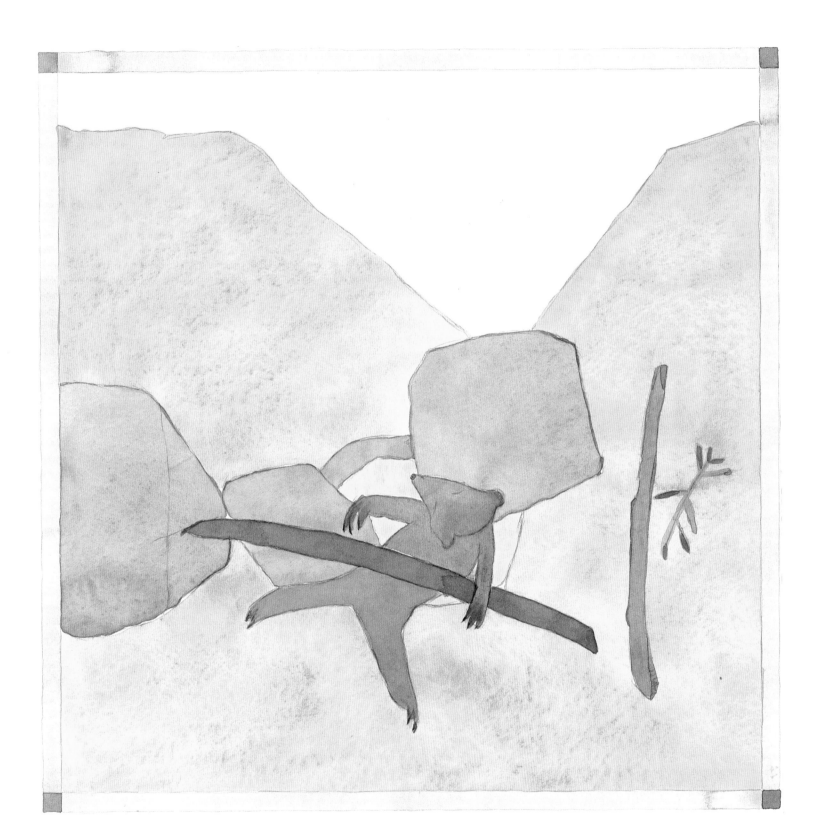

Let

us not

be

tempted,

but

deliver

us

from our

enemy:

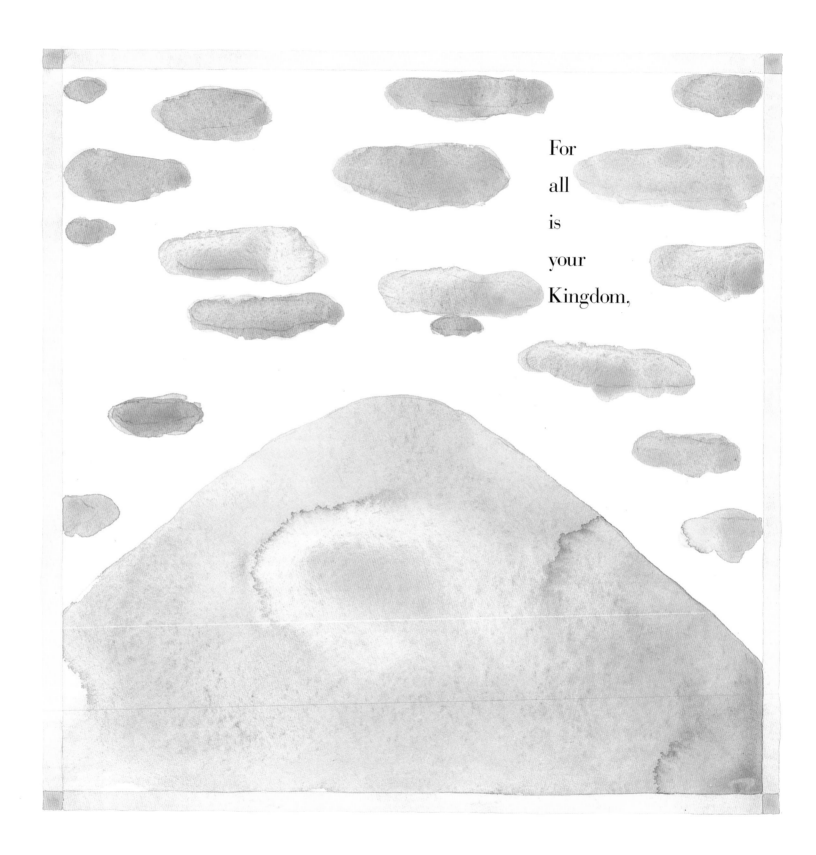

For

all

is

your

Kingdom,

and

your

strength,

and

your

harmony,

forever.

Amen.